A
CRACK
IN THE
CLOUDS

and Other Poems

Also by Constance Levy

I'm Going To Pet a Worm Today and Other Poems
illustrated by Ronald Himler

A Tree Place and Other Poems
illustrated by Robert Sabuda

When Whales Exhale and Other Poems
illustrated by Judy LeBrasca

Margaret K. McElderry Books

A
CRACK
IN THE
CLOUDS

and Other Poems

Constance Levy

illustrations by

Robin Bell Corfield

Margaret K. McElderry Books

Margaret K. McElderry Books
An imprint of Simon & Schuster
Children's Publishing Division
1230 Avenue of the Americas
New York, New York 10020

Book design by Nina Barnett
The text of this book is set in Bembo.
The illustrations are rendered in pen and ink.
Printed and bound in the United States of America
First Edition
10 9 8 7 6 5 4 3 2 1
Library of Congress Cataloging-in-Publication Data
Levy, Constance.
A crack in the clouds and other poems / Constance
Levy; illustrations by Robin Bell Corfield.—1st ed.
p.   cm.
Summary: A collection of thirty-eight original poems
about the natural world.
ISBN 0-689-82204-9
1. Nature—Juvenile poetry. 2. Children's poetry,
American. [1. Nature—Poetry. 2. American poetry.]
I. Corfield, Robin Bell, ill. II. Title.
PS3562.E9256C72   1998
811'.54—dc21   98-10652

To Bob, Carol, Ken, Don, Ed, Marjie,
Bernie, Cyndee, Hedva, and Joelyn
—C.L.

Contents

Hot Feet on the Beach   1

Run from the Waves!   2

Shadow Fish   3

Cricket Nights   4

Hide and Beep   5

Rabbit Barber   6

On the Fourth of July   7

Corn Smiles   8

Iced Feet   9

Herb Garden   10

The Pond   11

A Very Big Spiderweb   12

Schedule   13

Water Sounds   14

Bur   15

Jack-o'Lantern   16

A Comet Named Hale-Bopp   17

City Slipper   18

White and Red   19

Making Icicles   20

Icicles!	21
Spring Watch	22
To a Luna Moth Fresh from Her Cocoon	23
Streetwise Weeds	24
Wren at Work	25
Rain at the Night Game	26
A Crack in the Clouds	27
Cowscape	28
Bike Down!	29
Interview with a Dog	30
The Wrecking Machine	31
To the New Baby Elephant	32
Seagull Tricks	33
Misty	34
At the Ballet	35
Unknown Places	36
A Tree Fell	37
Feet Talk	38
Index of First Lines	40

Hot Feet on the Beach

Bare feet,
be smart;
there's solar fire
baked into
each grain of sand.
Too burning hot
for standing flat!

Dig down;
you'll find
a hidden cache
of ocean cool
to beat the heat.

Even
cherrystone clams
know
that!

Run from the Waves!

Scream!
Run from the sea dragon's
wrath;
be quick!
Let it lick
no more than your
sandcaked heel.
Tease it till
it falls at your feet
docile and meek,
a slurping tongue
slipping back to the sea.

But don't relax;
it's coming back.
Scream,
run!

Shadow Fish

A still pool of summer sun
beside a sleepy tree,
ho hum . . .

A sudden breeze
makes leaves swish,
waking lively
shadow fish;
try catching some!

Cricket Nights

All night
they tune
their violins,
all night
that steady
humming din,
and all night long
I wish that they
would learn to play
at least ONE song!

Hide and Beep

Tree frog,
I see you in my flashlight beam,
puffed close to popping
like a small balloon,

beeping in the yew bush,
honking like a horn,
swelling and yelling.
What are you telling?
Who are you calling
with your hiccup of song,
drowning out the crickets
all this summer night long?

Rabbit Barber

This weeping willow
used to be
my favorite place to hide.
The branches flowing
to the ground
made a sort of cave inside—

until that little barber came,
a furry one in brownish gray,
who nibbled, nibbled all around
about an inch per branch each day.

And though he trimmed it evenly
and made it nice and neat,
it's much too short!
Now anyone who looks
can see my feet.

On the Fourth of July

Wow, a flare of silver wiggles!
Oh, a waterfall of red!
Now, two purple skyflowers blooming
high in the darkness
overhead!

The sky is bright with starbursts
falling
gold and blue and green,
as I
hear my little brother calling,
"LOOK, in the grass,
a FIREFLY!"

Corn Smiles

Gift–wrapped
in pea green covering,
fresh from the cornfield
and warm from the sun,
my brimming bag
of summer corn . . .

I pick up an ear
and peek inside.
Surprise!
Corn teeth
in the widest grin,

and me
smiling back
the same
at them.

Iced Feet

A mountain stream
to cross—
let's go!

It's not very deep,
not very wide.
We toss our shoes
to the other side,
stuff our socks
in our pockets, try
wading in to our ankle tops.

Oh, it's frosty cold
and we slip in the mud
and we teeter on the rocks,
but no one stops,

because summer feet
in the crisp, the sweet,
delicious rush
of melting snows
don't care
if they have
frozen toes!

Herb Garden

Rub a mint leaf
in your fingers;
notice how the fragrance
lingers.
Pick a fennel seed
and chew it;
you'll think "licorice"
as you do it.
Fill your pocket
with sweet basil.
Make a sage and thyme bouquet.
Slip in some oregano,
and you'll be
totally
"gourmet"!

The Pond

The pond is a dark green mirror
that captures a bit of sky,
but something is hiding
that you should see
if you are passing by.

Bubbles rise up, and underneath,
with quick little darts and glides,
tadpoles wiggle their fish tails
and bracelets of white eggs slide

and there through a maze of tangles
like a shadowy forest of ferns,
a frog in his secret garden
frog-kicks
and stretches
and turns.

A Very Big Spiderweb

Look what's
hanging out to dry,
a beautiful thing
to discover:
spanning two trees,
lacy and round,
a tablecloth
for a manhole cover!

Schedule

Here's how spiders
plan their day:
work and wait
work and wait.
Spiders never hesitate;
when there's work
they don't wait.

When it's spinning time
they spin.
Time for mending? They begin
right away
closing gaps
and they never pause for naps.

When their schedule
tells them "wait,"
they don't stop to celebrate,
but they wait
the way they work,
very keenly on alert.
We could learn a thing or two,
sticking to it as they do.

Water Sounds

When it's quiet in the forest
as I'm hiking to explore
far away from city places
where no noisy engines roar,

where electric sounds are insects
and the neighbors talk like birds,

the trickle, trickle,
whoosh and *plink*
of rushing water
is, I think,
the best song

ever heard.

Bur

I picked off
a bur,
a sticky
bur
that clutched my shirt,

a pod
of seeds
with an urge
to travel
but no wings to fly
that hitchhiked
a ride,

hopping on board
from the weeds
near the road
as my sleeve
brushed by.

Well, seeds in need
do have to try!

Jack-o'-Lantern

From the field
I was chosen
because
I am squat
and charmingly fat,
the pride of the patch
in my bright pumpkin orange,
and you can't be any
oranger than that.

Yet now, I don't know . . .
I'm not what I was,
though I feel a glow
from my crown to my chin.
Why must I wear this
brainless grin?
Why such
an empty feeling within?
Is it that thing
they call
Hollow-een?

A Comet Named Hale-Bopp
(1997)

This ancient ball
of ice and gas
and cosmic grit,
this once-in-a-lifetime
visitor from outer space
is here,
clear
and luminous.

The sight of it
is my dessert
tonight:
part spot of silver-white,
part misty swallowtail,
almost a moon
among the stars
but
not
quite.

City Slipper

White snow
turned gray.
The fluff
is slush,
and all the curbs
where plows
have pushed the snow
wear dark mustaches.
Streets may
have something
up their sleeves;
beware of
slick
ice patches!

White and Red

Old squirrel nests
are igloos now.
Snow muffins line
the spruce and pine.
The fierce wind howls
at five below,
but hot red holly berries shine!

It's winter's world:
white underfoot
and white sky overhead,
and a robin keeping his tummy warm
eating holly berry red.

Making Icicles

To snowbound roofs
the sun comes calling,
and gutters and eaves
go water-falling.

Then sun leaves.
There's a shivery freeze,

and the water's stalling

right there

in
mid
  a
  i
  r
  !

Icicles!

Hooray!
Icicles are everywhere today:
ice spikes,
sharks' teeth,
sleek frost fingers,

and the mailbox
wears a fringe
of winter splinters!

Spring Watch

As tight as misers
grip their gold,
that's the way
these leaf buds hold.

They loosen such a stingy bit
each day, I barely notice it.

Snow has melted.
Dry creeks flow.
The calender says NOW, but no
little fists of green unfold.

The springing out of spring is
s   l   o   w!

To a Luna Moth Fresh from Her Cocoon

Night princess,
It is dusk now.
Let me look
a little longer
as you smooth
the folds and wrinkles
and your weak new wings
grow stronger.
Let me watch the green silk
flowing from
your purple-collared cape.
Do not hurry.
Let me love you
till the moon
steals you away.

Streetwise Weeds

I like those weeds
of sturdy stock
that push through
sidewalks, brick and rock.
They say,
  "Concrete?
  No problem there!"
and find a crack
as thin as hair,
squeeze right in
and up they go.

They have no fear
of heat or snow
or cars or feet;
they persevere
because they really
want to grow.

Wren at Work

Wren at work;
look at her,
the happy little
carpenter.
Up to her cup-shaped nest
she brings
a beakful of
new-home furnishings.
But then,
before she gathers more,
she flies to a nearby branch
and sings!

What's inside?
Peek and see:
grass for softness,
feathers for love,
twigs to hold it
safe and snug,
three larvae,
two small snails,
one round black bug.

Nice house
to grow up in
if you're a
baby wren.

Rain at the Night Game

Light rain
at the night game;
diamonds from the dark

filter through the lights
of the baseball park,

twinkle past the upper deck
like sparkle-studded lace.

From row 15
behind third base,
this ballpark is
a magic place!

A Crack in the Clouds

How could
one slight
slit,
just a tiny bit
of a crack
in the cover
of clouds,
permit
such a pouring of sun
that engulfs
E V E R Y O N E ?

Cowscape

Six grazing cows
posing
as we pass

　white cow　　　brown cow

　　brown and white　　white cow

　　　white cow
　　　　　brown cow

all chewing grass.

Bike Down!

After
the ride up
that pulls hard
at your legs,
sucks
your breath
to desert-dry,

celebrate!

Speed down
as the wind
fills your hair
with wild air,
and the pedals
don't even need
your feet,
and you

FLY !

Interview with a Dog

I'm a mysterious dog,
true to my master
but cunning,
off with the first
light of dawn
eager and running,

rousing the quail
from the brush,
pursuing
a rabbit,
bending a path
in the wet
morning grass,
shaking
a shower
of dew as I pass.
This is my habit.

They gave me a name
and I come
when they call,
but they don't really
know me at all
because
I'm
a
mysterious
dog.

The Wrecking Machine
(good-bye to the house next door)

It charges the house
like an angry bull;
this long-necked
high-lift wrecking machine.
It butts and it bites
and it crushes and chomps,
and it whacks its chin
and the roof caves in.
(Oh, it looks mean!)

Dust floats around it
thick as smoke.
It lifts its head
and with one poke
down go windows,
a door,
a wall,
glass panes shatter,
bricks
fall.

It snorts!
It squeals!
The engine drones
as it scoops up its bounty
of old house bones.

To the New Baby Elephant

I see how your soft pink trunk
curls at the tip like a snail,
how it scoops up
a hank of hay
   that
     slips
       away,

how a playful kick
tips over your pail
spilling water
   across
      the gray
        cement . . .
Oh, baby,
you've so much to learn

about being an
elephant!

Seagull Tricks

You may think
he's not thinking
about your sandwich
because he is looking
the other way.

You may think
he's not scheming
because he is dreaming
and stands like an innocent
statue in gray.

And the place where he lands,
which is three feet away,
seems a safe enough spot.
Well, I warn you, it's not.

You will soon be
"un-sandwiched"
as I was today!

Misty

Old alley cat
likes the morning mist,
when everything
seems
as gray
as his fur
and the neighborhood
looks mysterious.

Softness follows him
as he walks,
around the trash can,
over the stoop,
licking the air
delicious with scents
and rich
as mulligatawny soup.

At the Ballet

Now I

know

that legs have

wings

and arms are

petals of

a thousand

different

flowers.

Unknown Places

We are crossing the river
to another city
in a different state

over a bridge
where lanes spin off
and signs
with names and numbers wait,

each one saying
in bright white letters
on tempting green:
"Follow *ME*
to unknown places."
"Left," they urge,
or "Right,"
or "Try the exit lane."

But we follow our map
so we don't slip up.
We *know* where we're going.

I wonder, though,
what we miss,

always knowing . . .

A Tree Fell

A graceful giant
is lying there.

Cars edge around it.
People stare.
They see
a ponderous trunk
with tousled leaves,

a muddy nub
of roots
laid bare.

What happened
last night
in the storm?
Did anyone hear
the awful thud?

Feet Talk

Listen as your feet
tell you where they walk:
    gravel crackles,
    grass squeaks,
    sneaker slaps
    on hard concrete.
Tune in to
    friendly chitchat
    of feet meeting feet:
    hurried shuffles, clacks, thumps
    crossing busy streets.
Hear your feet talk
street talk!

Index of First Lines

A graceful giant   37
A mountain stream   9
A still pool of summer sun   3
After   29
All night   4
As tight as misers   22

Bare feet,   1

From the field   16

Gift-wrapped   8

Here's how spiders   13
Hooray!   21
How could   27

I like those weeds   24
I picked off   15
I see how your soft pink
   trunk   32
I'm a mysterious dog,   30
It charges the house   31

Light rain   26
Listen as your feet   38
Look what's   12

Night princess,   23
Now I   35

Old alley cat   34
Old squirrel nests   19

Rub a mint leaf   10

Scream!   2
Six grazing cows   28

The pond is a dark green
   mirror   11
This ancient ball   17
This weeping willow   6
To snowbound roofs   20
Tree frog,   5

We are crossing the river   36
When it's quiet in the forest   14
White snow   18
Wren at work;   25
Wow, a flare of silver wiggles!   7

You may think   33